BETWEEN THE PAGES

MONET POUSSAY

JUST HER STORIES
PUBLISHING

A SMALL FAVOR

A Small Favor Before You Begin

If you're reading this through Kindle Unlimited, authors like me are paid by the pages you read. One simple way you can support Indie authors is by scrolling to the end of the book before you start reading. It ensures that your reading progress is fully tracked, and it really helps us out.

Thank you so much for your support. I hope you enjoy the story!

Cover Art by DaNeal Eberly of Art by DaNeal

Cover Design by D' Arte Oriel https://www.darteoriel.com

Edited by Amanda Burbank

eBook ISBN: 979-8-9932383-1-9

First Edition: 2025

Published by Just Her Stories Publishing

www.justherstories.com

Disclaimer: This book contains mature themes, language, and content that may not be suitable for all readers. Reader discretion is advised.

❋ Formatted with Vellum

For DaNeal -
My heart, my home, and my reason to keep writing, who
reminds me that love is both anchor and fire.
To my Friends -
Thank you for holding space for the story, and for me.
And to my Editor, Amanda Burbank -
Your insight, care, and honesty helped shape this book into
something I'm proud of.

CAST OF CHARACTERS

Siobhan Kelly

A sharp-witted book editor with a guarded heart who's better with words on a page than the ones spoken aloud. Siobhan lives by deadlines and coffee refills, but beneath the polish is a woman craving connection. She never expected a virtual friendship to become something more, something real.

Jessica Monroe

A social worker at a small community center, Jessica spends her days helping others find stability, something she's still learning to give herself. Compassionate, grounded, and quietly brave, she carries the weight of others' stories... until one weekend in the pines begins to rewrite her own.

CHAPTER 1

I wasn't planning on talking to anyone that morning. That was kind of the point: wake up early, drive into town, drink something hot while pretending to read a book I'd already read twice. Keep my head down. To blend in.

That little shop on Main Street was supposed to be forgettable. Another overdecorated café where someone decided books and bouquets made coffee taste better. But it was warm, and the Wi-Fi worked, and no one seemed in a rush to kick you out. I could live with that.

"You're new around here."

The voice was soft but direct, and it cut through the mental list I was reciting about which type of pasta was the best. Jessica loved pasta. I looked up.

She wasn't even really looking at me, not yet. Just leaned against the counter, her arms crossed in a relaxed way that said she belonged here as if this place was her second skin.

"Is it that obvious?" I asked, offering a smile that was more reflexive than an invitation.

She glanced at me, one eyebrow raised. "You hesitated before ordering. That's how we can tell."

I gave a small laugh, mostly out of habit. "Maybe I'm just indecisive."

She tilted her head, a grin playing at the edge of her mouth. "Then I won't tell you we have six syrups and three types of milk. It might break you."

I cracked a genuine smile at that. Not because it was especially funny, but because it felt easy. The way she said it, light, effortless, like breathing. I ordered a plain coffee. No room, no extras. Nothing that might slow me down. She didn't ask my name, and I didn't ask hers.

But I did glance back at her as I walked out, just briefly.

She was wiping the counter, laughing with the older woman who'd ordered before me. The kind of laugh that sounded like it happened a lot around her.

She fit here. That much was obvious. She was

like a piece of this small-town puzzle that didn't have to keep trying to find its place.

I wasn't jealous. Not exactly. Just… curious. I couldn't remember the last time I'd slipped into a place and felt like I belonged there. Like, I didn't have to earn it. Like, I didn't have to tuck away a few pieces of myself first.

I pushed open the café door, the little bell above it chiming like it had a secret to tell. The cold hit my cheeks as I stepped outside, the warmth of the coffee in my hands grounding me more than I cared to admit.

My mind was filled with anticipation for this weekend. *Would things be the same in person?* For weeks, we'd traded looks, screen to screen, late-night messages, and occasional voice notes that felt like stolen pieces of something we both wanted more of.

And now she was coming.

By the time I climbed into my Jeep, my stomach was a knot of nerves and low-burning anticipation. The place was already tidy, the fresh sheets tucked in with hotel-level precision. I'd stocked the fridge with three kinds of juice, two kinds of hummus, and one wild guess at her favorite chocolate. A nervous grocery haul, basically.

The road back to the cabin curved gently through the trees, dusted in snow and quiet in a way that always made me feel like the world was on pause. I had one hand on the wheel, the other wrapped around the to-go cup I hadn't touched yet. The coffee was probably cold by now, but I didn't care.

I kept thinking about her. About Jessica.

Not in that tentative, hopeful way I used to when we first started messaging. Back then, she was just words on a screen, a voice note played too many times, a picture saved to my phone that I looked at more than I'd admit. But this, now, it felt different. Closer. It was like something real had started growing in the quiet spaces between us.

I could picture her in the passenger seat. One boot tucked under her knee, scarf falling slightly off one shoulder, talking about something small that mattered more than she realized. She had a way of telling stories as if she wasn't sure they were worth sharing, and somehow they always were.

She'd told me bits and pieces about her life. Her sister called twice a week like clockwork. Her mom was doing better now, but hadn't always. Her job at the community center and how she kept granola bars in her desk drawer for the hungry kids.

She didn't act like any of that made her brave. But it did. It made her solid in a way that didn't feel heavy. Steady but soft.

And somewhere between mile marker eight and the old gas station sign that never lit up, I realized something I hadn't let myself say before.

She wouldn't just fit into my life.

She'd *belong* in it.

It wasn't as if she'd shrunk herself down to fit into the quiet routines I'd built. It's not like she had to earn her place. She'd *fit* the way light fits into a room when you finally pull the curtain back.

I didn't know what that meant yet. Not exactly.

But for the first time in a long time, I didn't feel like I had to run from the feeling.

I just wanted to see where it could go.

The dirt road crunched under my tires as I pulled up to the Airbnb.

It's a cute little cabin in the pines. It was not much, just two rooms, a sloped roof, and a porch that creaked when the wind so much as looked at it, but it had what we needed. A fireplace, a sturdy desk, and enough solitude to make it easy to avoid my phone and concentrate on Jessica and me.

I dropped my car keys into the basket by the door and let the silence of the cabin settle around me. It was the kind of quiet I usually craved, uninterrupted and absolute, but tonight, it felt different. Tonight, it felt like the breath before something exciting began.

I threw some logs in the fireplace and tossed in a match. Beautiful. Jessica will like that.

I set the coffee down on the desk, opened my journal, and sat for a moment, just listening to the wind against the windows. Then I started to write.

She's coming today.

Jessica. After weeks of messages, voice notes, and the occasional midnight "Are you still awake?" text, we're actually going to be in the same room.

It's strange how something can feel familiar and utterly new at the same time. I know the sound of her laugh. I know that she has a habit of rambling when she's nervous and that she reads the last page of a book before the first. But I don't know what it'll be like to stand next to her. To watch her smile in real-time. To see the way she takes up space when she's not just a voice in my ear.

I paused, the pen tapping gently against the edge of the page.

Part of me is terrified. What if it's awkward? What if we don't fit the way we did on screen? What if I ruin it?

But there's another part of me, quieter, steadier, that's hopeful. She's already seen the pieces of me I usually hide. The sarcasm, the distance, the way I disappear when things get too real. And she's still coming.

Work is manageable. Another piece is due Monday, something about small-town tourism. Irony noted. Becca texted to remind me that I "still suck at returning calls," and Maya sent a GIF of someone hyperventilating into a paper bag, which I assume was her way of wishing me good luck. I should probably tell them both I'm not spiraling. Not yet.

I've done a lot of leaving in my life. This is the first time I've stayed still long enough for someone to find me.

And she did.

I underlined that last sentence slowly.

Then I closed my journal and looked toward the front door, half expecting a knock, even though it was still hours too early.

Still, I couldn't help but feel it.

Hope.

And for once, I didn't try to write it away.

Wood. We need some firewood.

I stepped out onto the porch, the old screen door creaking behind me, and pulled my jacket tighter against the chill. The air was sharp and clean, the kind of cold that woke you up without asking permission. A low stack of un-split logs sat just beyond the edge of the cabin, half-frosted and waiting. I crunched across the frosty ground toward them, boots pressing patterns into the earth, breath clouding in front of me like smoke. It wasn't about the fire. I'd already built one. This was about nerves. About giving my body something to do while my mind kept drifting to a car that hadn't pulled up yet and a woman I'd only ever seen through a screen.

I split the first log clean in half, the sound sharp and satisfying in the cold morning air. The rhythm helped lift, drop, crack, repeat, something steady to do with my hands while my mind tried not to count down the minutes.

The pile grew, but it didn't make the wait feel shorter. If anything, it made it more real. She was on her way. Every swing of the axe echoed with *she's really coming*. And despite myself, I was starting to hope the fire wouldn't be the only thing keeping us warm tonight.

I had never liked waiting, but there was something different about this waiting.

The kind where I'm not sure if I'm about to meet the love of my life or a really expensive mistake.

The scent of fresh-cut pine lingered sharply in the air, mingling with the colder, deeper smell of damp earth and old leaves. Every swing of the axe kicked up another breath of resin, clean, bright, almost sweet, while wood chips scattered at my boots like splinters of sunlight. The trees stood tall around me, still and watching, their needles whispering overhead in the wind. The cabin sat just behind me, smoke curling gently from the chimney, and everything else was quiet except for the rhythmic thud of the blade and the occasional creak of branches shifting in the shadows.

I adjusted the last log on the firewood stack and

stepped back to assess it: neatly arranged, symmetrical, and solid. That's how I liked things. Organized. Predictable. Except nothing about this trip was that. Jessica wasn't predictable. Not in messages, not on late-night video calls. And definitely not in the way she made me feel like I was seventeen again every time my phone lit up with her name.

The low hum of tires over gravel pulled my attention toward the winding driveway. Headlights flickered between the trees. I wiped my hands off on my jeans and reached for the axe out of habit, setting it against the porch rail. I pulled off my gloves, shoved them into my coat pocket, and stood with my boots planted wide, my heart beating steadily but too loudly.

The Subaru came to a stop. The engine cut off.

And then I saw her.

Jessica stepped out like a flame in the middle of all that forest. She was wrapped in an oversized orange coat and wearing a smile that could disarm a bear. Smaller than I expected, but somehow larger than life. Her eyes scanned the cabin and the porch and then landed on me.

"Hey!" she called out, waving like they weren't meeting in person for the very first time.

I nodded and raised a hand, a slow half-smile tugging at my mouth. "Hey."

Jessica crossed the gravel with an uncertain bounce in her step, dragging a suitcase behind her. Her scarf was half undone, and her hair whipped by the wind.

It started with a hug.

Not one of those stiff, side-arm, polite things either. Jessica wrapped her arms around me like it wasn't the first time. Like we hadn't spent weeks dancing around a screen trying to be casual while secretly over-analyzing every emoji.

"You're taller than I thought," she said against my shoulder.

"I get that a lot," I replied, trying not to sound like I was panicking on the inside. "Most people assume I'm five-six and emotionally unavailable."

She laughed. *Thank God.*

"You're brighter," I replied before I could stop myself. My voice came out low, a little rougher than intended.

Jessica blinked and then laughed. "Brighter? Like a lightbulb?"

"Like the sun."

Jessica grinned, and I realized she'd meant it more than she thought.

"I brought wine," Jessica said, lifting a paper bag with both hands like it might break if she held it wrong.

I took it from her, fingers brushing briefly. Warm. Soft. "Good. I didn't bring anything fancy."

"I like simple," Jessica said, stepping past her onto the porch.

So do I, I wanted to say. But there was nothing simple about the way Jessica moved through the door like she belonged.

Inside, the fire burned steadily. I had made sure of that, anything to keep busy while I waited. The cabin was small but clean. Worn-in furniture, thick curtains, the scent of cedar, and something sweet on the walls. She liked places like this. Quiet, old, unbothered.

Jessica turned in a slow circle. "This is beautiful. It feels warm, cozy... I like it."

"I figured that'd be good," I said, setting the wine on the counter.

"It looks like it's going to warm up a bit this weekend."

Jessica looked at her over her shoulder. "You always talk like you're predicting the weather."

I shrugged. "I read the signs."

Our eyes lingered. That part hadn't changed.

Online, they always found excuses to stare too long. Now, there was no screen, no buffer. Just two people with too many questions and too little time.

"And that?" she pointed toward the closed door down the hall.

"Ah, yes. The cabin's most mysterious chamber, the bathroom."

I finally nodded toward the hallway. "Bedrooms down there. One queen bed. I can take the couch."

Jessica tilted her head. "Do I look like the kind of girl who'd let you sleep on a couch after chopping firewood like a damn lumberjack?"

That made me smile. "You don't look like the kind of girl I can argue with."

"Exactly."

Jessica disappeared down the hallway with a bounce in her step, dragging her suitcase like it was nothing. I followed slower, wine glass in hand, each step feeling heavier than it should have.

The bedroom door creaked open.

She stopped just inside.

"Oh," she said.

I stepped up behind her and looked past her shoulder. Just like the listing said, there was a queen bed, nightstands on either side, and a window that overlooked the lake. What it didn't mention was how small the room actually was, the kind of small where shoulders might brush even if you were trying not to touch.

I leaned a shoulder into the doorframe, arms crossed, trying to play it cool. "Didn't realize it was only one bed until I got here."

She turned to face me, her expression unreadable. "Siobhan…"

"It's fine," I added too quickly. "It's just three nights."

She tilted her head and narrowed her eyes in the way she does when she's not buying it. I've seen that look on Zoom calls and over photos of sunsets. It hits harder in person. "You always do that."

"Do what?"

"Make decisions for people without asking if they want something different."

I blinked. "I just don't want you to be uncomfortable."

Her voice softened, but it didn't lose its edge. "I'm not."

I looked away. The edge of the dresser caught my eye, with worn wood and scratches on the top like someone had once dropped a bag too hard, anything to focus on besides her eyes.

"I'm just trying to respect boundaries," I mumbled.

Jessica stepped closer. I could feel the heat of her even before she touched me.

"I came here because I wanted to be close to you," she said. "Not just emotionally."

I swallowed. "Space-wise, huh?"

She laughed quietly, and I felt it in my ribs. "Exactly. And I'm fine with sharing unless you snore."

"I don't."

"Then we're fine."

She walked over to the bed and casually dropped her body onto it like she'd done it a thousand times before. Her scarf trailed behind her, half-falling off the edge of the mattress. She stretched her arms out dramatically and sank into the thick navy comforter.

"This might be the most comfortable thing I've ever lain on," she said, eyes closed, grinning.

I hesitated, still standing like a statue in the doorway.

Then, finally, I sat down on the edge of the mattress.

The bed dipped beneath me, her body shifting slightly with the movement. Our knees brushed, just barely, but I felt it like a live wire.

"Still okay?" I asked, my voice lower than I meant it to be.

Jessica turned her head to look at me, her face soft. "I think this whole trip just started to feel real."

"Yeah." I could barely say it out loud. "It feels that way."

We stayed like that for a moment, knee to knee, heartbeats humming just out of sync. I didn't reach for her. I wanted to. My fingers twitched with it. But I didn't.

I've always believed closeness should be earned, not assumed.

Jessica shifted slightly and looked up at the ceiling. "You don't have to keep your distance. Not unless you want to."

I turned my hand palm up on the bed between us. Just enough.

She slid her fingers across the blanket until they touched mine.

"I don't want to," I said.

CHAPTER 2

We unpacked in fits and starts; Jessica moved like a whirlwind while I was a slow shadow beside her. When we met in the kitchen, there was laughter. Nervous, but real. Jessica was pouring her second glass of wine before I had finished my first glass.

Dinner was shrimp and pasta because I wanted something easy, and I couldn't mess up garlic and oil without actively trying. She offered to help, and twenty minutes later, we were sharing counter space, grating cheese, and pretending not to be nervous.

"So," Jessica said, sliding a pot toward me, "is this where you usually bring women from the internet?"

I looked at her deadpan. "Yes. Every weekend. It's part of my time-share cult initiation."

She blinked. I let it hang for a beat before grinning.

"Okay, you can't say stuff like that with a straight face," she said, nudging me with her hip. "I almost believed you."

I shrugged. "I'm very persuasive. It's a Sagittarius thing."

We were lying on the couch, legs tangled, my hand resting lightly on her stomach as she traced invisible shapes on my arm. The fire had burned down to soft embers, and the world outside the cabin was pitch dark. In what had to be the most awkwardly silent twenty seconds of my life, I blurted, "This is weird, right? Not *bad*, weird. Just... two people who've only heard each other snore through walls, weird."

She gave me a look. "I haven't even heard you snore yet."

"Oh, just wait. It's like a haunted vacuum. Sexy, right?"

"Honestly, I'm just impressed by your confidence. Wait, you said you didn't snore."

That broke the tension. Or maybe it was already breaking, and I'd just been too anxious to notice.

We didn't talk about anything dramatic that night. No big reveals. Just quiet things, movies we half-remembered, places we'd been, foods we hated. She hated olives. I tried not to judge.

But the real shift came somewhere between her laughter and the way she tucked her legs under herself like she'd done it a hundred times on this couch.

Jessica tilted her head toward me. "Can I ask you something?"

I nodded. "Always."

Her voice was soft and thoughtful. "What are you most grateful for right now?"

I didn't answer right away. My mind flickered through a dozen things: small comforts, big fears, the sound of her laugh, the feel of her body pressed against mine under layers of blankets.

But what I said was true.

"You," I whispered. "Not just being here, but choosing to come. When I got quiet and scared, you stayed. I appreciate you standing by me."

She smiled, slow and quiet. Her fingers moved to brush the side of my face.

"I never felt like I was choosing," she said. "It just... felt right."

I let the silence linger before I asked, "And you? What are you most grateful for?"

Jessica didn't hesitate.

"Being seen," she said. "Really seen. Without having to explain myself. You make me feel like I'm enough, just like this."

I pulled her closer and kissed her forehead.

"You are," I said. "Exactly like this."

We didn't speak again for a long time.

But in the space between our words, I could feel everything that mattered most.

Jessica looked over. "I still can't believe I'm here with you, Siobhan."

I studied her, taking in the curve of her cheek and the soft shine in her eyes. "I can."

Jessica smiled, a little shy this time. "Yeah?"

"Yeah."

The wine was half-gone, and both our feet were tucked under the same blanket.

Jessica leaned into me, her head on my shoulder. Our bodies curved into each other as if the shape had been there, waiting to be found. Her fingers idly circled the rim of her glass while mine rested around her waist.

The fire cracked now and then, soft and low. No music, no TV. Just this. Just us.

She sighed, content. "You ever notice how quiet the world gets when it's not trying to prove anything?"

I glanced down at her. "That's you. You quiet the whole room when you walk in."

She laughed, burying her face against my collarbone. "You always say things like that when I'm not ready."

"That's the point," I murmured.

She leaned back, looking up at me, wine-catching firelight in her glass. "What?"

I hesitated.

Then I reached down and grabbed the folded piece of paper from between the couch cushions, which I had slipped there earlier when I almost lost my nerve. Again.

"I wrote you something," I said, careful with the words, like they might break.

Jessica blinked. "Like… a poem?"

She shifted, pulling back just enough to search my face, eyebrows raised. "You were writing about me before you even met me?"

I nodded. "Don't say anything—
not until it's over."

Her heartbeat slowed beneath my hand.

She set her wine glass aside, quiet now, waiting.

"Okay."

I unfolded the paper and smoothed the crease against my leg.

She knew I loved slam poetry, the rhythm, the rise and fall,

the way a poem is meant to be *heard* as much as read.

And in that moment, the air shifted.

The room hushed, like even the walls were waiting.

Her eyes on me, steady, unblinking, my only audience.

So when I began, I didn't just read.

I performed.

> I met you
> —in the glow of a screen.
> Pixels carrying pieces of your soul.
> Your voice...
> slid into my nights like honey,
> like a secret the stars were desperate
> to overhear.
> We talked until the moon got tired.
> Our screens lit each other's faces—
> a universe where it was only

you,
and me,
and laughter spilling past 2 a.m,
like we were building a bridge
one giggle at a time.
And now—
I imagine your skin.
Warm beneath my fingertips.
Velvet, woven from every story you've
told.

The answer to questions
my body's been whispering
for years.
I want to kiss you.
Not just lips.
But the kindness you carry,
the curves of your care,
the soft edges of your love.
Because your beauty—
it isn't surface.
It's wildfire.
It begins in your chest.
Roars in your heart.
Spills into the world

every time you choose others
before yourself.
And when we meet—
when the distance folds into nothing,
I want my gift to be more than
ribbon,
more than paper.
I want it to be—
my eyes, holding yours steady.
My arms, becoming your safe place.
My lips, speaking the language
words will never hold.
Because you…
are beautiful.
Inside.
And out.
And I—
I am already falling.
Not into a screen.

I pause. My voice softens.

But into you.

I wasn't breathing. Not really.

The words had left my mouth, but they still hung in the air like smoke. My fingers clenched the paper tighter than I meant to. The fire popped once, but even that didn't break the silence.

Jessica hadn't said a word.

She just stared at me like she wasn't sure whether to speak or cry.

And then she moved.

She straddled my lap, slow and certain, like gravity had been pulling her there all along. Her knees pressed into my hips, her arms sliding around my neck, heat radiating through every inch of her. Her eyes, when they met mine, were glassy and burning straight through me.

"You wrote that before you even touched me," she said.

I nodded, throat tight, breath catching when her chest brushed mine. "Yeah."

Her fingers brushed my face, soft and slow.

"You imagined me before you ever met me. And still, you wrote me like I was worth keeping."

I didn't know what to say. I'd never been good with words *after* I'd written them down.

Jessica leaned her forehead to mine, her breath warm and steady.

"You didn't write me like a firework," she whispered. "You wrote me like firelight. Like something soft. Something constant."

I swallowed hard, my hands coming to rest at her waist, holding her like she might disappear if I blinked too fast.

She pulled back just far enough to look at me, really look at me.

"That's the first time I've ever felt written," she said. "Not described. *Known.*"

Then she kissed me.

And it was everything. No spark, no explosion. Just heat and home, and this terrifying, beautiful sense that I had found the one person who would never treat my silence like a threat.

When she pulled away, her fingers stayed tucked behind my neck, her body still wrapped around mine.

"Reread it sometime," she whispered. "Tomorrow. Next year. After we fight. After we make up. When we're old."

I blinked. "Why?"

Her smile broke through, tired and sincere.

"Because I'm going to carry that poem in my chest for the rest of my life."

I exhaled into the curve of her neck, holding her tighter.

And for the first time since reading it, I felt safe enough to believe it.

For the first time in a long time, I didn't feel like running from anything.

Not even myself.

CHAPTER 3

*T*he fire had burned down to a low, flickering cradle of embers. The kind of glow that made everything feel softer, even the silence.

Jessica had slid down from the couch and sat beside me now, shoulder to shoulder, a shared blanket draped around both our backs. Her leg pressed warm against mine, her scent, something floral and clean, curling into my lungs like it belonged there.

I haven't said much in the last ten minutes. I didn't know how to explain the feeling sitting in my chest: a mix of ache and awe like I'd waited too long to be this close to someone who felt this right.

"You always get this quiet?" she asked, her voice

low as if the fire might shatter if we spoke too loudly.

"Only when I don't want to ruin something," I said.

Jessica turned to look at me. "Do you think you could?"

I met her eyes, open, steady, waiting. "I don't want to find out."

She smiled, slow and soft. "Then don't."

For a long moment, we just sat like that. My fingers curled around the edge of the blanket, hers just inches away on the cushion between us. I could feel the heat rolling off her skin, the way her breath hitched when I leaned just slightly closer.

I raised my hand, slow and careful, brushing her hair behind her ear again, letting my fingers trail down along her jaw. She leaned into it.

"Can I kiss you?" I asked, my voice barely more than a breath.

Jessica didn't answer with words. She just closed the distance.

Her lips press against mine with a sweetness that catches me off guard. It isn't demanding. It isn't loud. It's soft, searching, like a question I already know the answer to.

And just like that, everything inside me goes quiet.

I kiss her again, softer this time, just a brush of lips. Then once more, longer, until her breath hitched and her fingers curled in the fabric of my shirt. My hand slid down, grazing her arm, finding her fingers. I tangled them with mine and squeezed.

We didn't rush. Her nose grazed mine, her lips feathered over my jaw, down to the corner of my mouth again. Every little touch felt like a question, and every time I answered by leaning closer.

My thumb traced her lower lip, and she kissed it, slow and deliberate. Heat coiled low in my stomach. The blanket slips from our shoulders, forgotten, but her warmth stays pressed against me.

For a long moment, we just breathed each other in, the air thick with everything waiting to happen. My pulse thrummed, not from impatience, but from knowing she wanted this too.

Without a word, I led her down the hallway, her fingers twined with mine. Every step felt too fast and too slow at once.

The bedroom is the same room it had always been, but with her beside me, it felt different now, warmer, charged, and alive. The shadows don't seem so long anymore; the silence hums like it's holding its breath.

We stopped at the foot of the bed and just stood there, the air thick with everything unsaid. Jessica's eyes searched mine as though she needed to be sure, needed me to show her this wasn't a mistake.

So I kissed her again. Not hurried, not greedy, slower this time, savoring the way her lips softened under mine, the way she melted closer. My hands found her waist; hers slid into my hair, fingertips trembling.

When I pulled back, only an inch, her breath brushed against my mouth. Neither of us spoke. My fingers traced the hem of her shirt, waiting, and she answered with a nod so slight it could have been imagined.

I took my time. Every button, every layer, slips away like a promise we've both been waiting to unwrap. Her hands mirrored mine, unhurried, reverent. The anticipation became its own kind of touch, each pause sharpening the next moment until the space between us burned hotter than the fire had. Every inch of skin we touched said what words hadn't.

I lay her down as she matters.

Because she did.

I've imagined this many times. And now it's happening. I felt Jessica's hand on my back, and everything became real as the cool night air hit my skin.

Jessica's eyes roam over my naked body, and a soft moan escapes my lips. I can't remember the last time anyone has ever looked at me the way she is right now. I feel shy and want to cover myself, but I stop and I let her eyes wander over my bare breasts.

My hand lies protectively on my stomach. Jessica pushes my hand away. My skin feels electric under her touch. Every inch of my skin that she touches burns. It's like a match in the dark, sudden and impossible to ignore. Her touch ignites my skin, every nerve remembering it was made to feel her.

Softly, Jessica's fingertips brush my cheek.

"You are so beautiful, Siobhan, it's actually distracting," Jessica says.

Whispering, I lean into her touch. "I only feel beautiful when you're touching me like this."

"That's because you are. Every inch of you... I want to worship."

I smile gently at her, my breath warm and gentle. "Then take your time; I'm all yours." I gently lift her hand to my mouth for a kiss. I kiss the back of her hand, then put two fingers in my mouth, licking and sucking them.

Jessica lets out a small moan. I didn't know how erotic that would feel, hearing that sound from her lips. My mouth is wet and hot around her fingers, and I can't help but imagine my mouth in other places on her.

The thought makes me push her back, and my hand releases hers, and it finds its way down her body and onto her thigh, pushing it out. My hand lingers on her thigh, stroking gently. Then, they find their way between her legs. Soft and damp, with want. The warmth there pulsed beneath my touch, drawing a sharp breath from both of us. It wasn't just the heat. It was the way her body responded, alive and trembling, as if it had been waiting for this moment, this exact connection. I let my hand linger, feeling the slick, fevered need of her body.

I pull my hand up to my mouth, licking my wet fingers. "I like the way you taste," I whisper.

Jessica's hands clamped down on the back of my thighs. Her warm breath is on my neck, her lips and mouth sucking and licking up to my chin.

My head swims with the sensation of her body against mine.

Jessica tilts her hips toward mine. I rest on my

elbows while my gaze roves down her body to between her legs. My lips stray over her breasts, my hand gently squeezing as my tongue traces and sucks her hard nipples. Jessica pushed my head closer to her, moaning softly.

I move my mouth lower, slowly, tasting every inch of her body. My lips grazed over her stomach and her thighs, and now hovered just above her heated skin. Her scent alone makes me dizzy. I softly flick my tongue out, tasting her and her softness, and then press in, slow and sure to savor every inch. The moan she let out was instant and trembling.

"You taste amazing."

I open my mouth wider, lips pressing into her tender flesh, sucking her clit gently, then my tongue goes deeper, drawing rhythm from instinct and desire. Every pull of my mouth and swirl of my tongue made Jessica's body arch closer, needier; I was devouring her, learning her by taste, and when I heard my name, "Siobhan," I gasped; I smiled and kept going. My rhythm deepens, tongue moving in slow, light, deliberate circles, then quick licks that send shudders rippling through her. I push a finger into her pussy and gently thrust it.

"More," she moaned. "I need more."

I slid another finger in, and her body trembled in

my hands. My long fingers filled her, pushing against her soft walls, pressing and rubbing in all the right places.

I curled my fingers, pressing against her wall, and she gasped.

"Oh, God," she moaned, "Siobhan, please, don't stop."

Jessica's fingers tangled in my hair, pulling, anchoring, as a cry broke loose, raw and breathless. Her pussy clenched my fingers, and her clit throbbed against my tongue. I didn't stop, not until her thighs, which were gripping my head, fell apart with a gasp that turned into a moan, her thighs trembling, her breath stolen.

I kissed her thighs gently, slowly, as Jessica regained her breath. Only then did I rise, lips wet and glistening. Jessica leaned up and, without a word, grabbed me and pulled me to her, kissed me deep, hungry, reverent. Our mouths met like fire and silk, the taste sweet, unmistakably hers. It was messy. Intimate. Real.

I couldn't breathe, not correctly, not with the way my body was unraveling underneath Jessica's tongue. Every stroke sent sparks along my spine, my thighs tightening around her shoulders, my hands lost in her soft hair. I tried to speak, to say her name, something, anything, but all that came was a gasp and a broken moan.

Her tongue was like velvet and heat, slow at first, teasing, making every one of my nerves hum with need. It licked lightly over me, then pressed deeper, firmer until pleasure surged through me like a rising tide. She focused on my clit, lightly and slowly, teasing me. Every movement was deliberate, as if she was savoring my taste and my reactions as they mattered. And it did. God, it did!

Then her fingers joined, two of them sliding in with such steady, aching care that my hips lifted on instinct. They were warm, slick, gentle, curling just right inside me, pressing into a place that made me cry out her name. The rhythm built, tongue stroking, fingers thrusting, circling, deepening, and my body couldn't tell what pressure was and what was pleasure anymore. It just was.

The pleasure built, thick and wild, and I could feel her fingers curl deep inside me. My hips arched, chasing every sweet pull of her lips, every deep kiss against the part of me that might shatter from too much feeling. And when the wave finally hit, it was blinding, my whole body trembling, clenching, burning as I moaned Jessica's name.

My thighs trembled, heat coiling tighter in my

core. It felt like being open in every way, physically, emotionally, completely, to someone who knew her body, even if they were still learning her soul. I barely had time to catch my breath before Jessica's lips were on my mouth, kissing me deeply. Our mouths moved in slow hunger, slick with the taste of my release. It was warm and earthy, and somehow sharing it made me feel even more bare, more wanted.

"I don't think there's anything sexier than tasting an orgasm on my lips."

She smiles and kisses me deeply.

Our breathing slowed together, syncing like tides settling after a storm. My body still pulsed with the echoes of pleasure, soft, warm waves that made me feel weightless and utterly spent. My skin was damp, and my heart was still fluttering, but it wasn't lust anymore. It was something quieter, something fuller.

I nestled into Jessica's chest, legs tangled beneath the covers, her skin against mine. Jessica's hand traced lazy circles on my back, grounding me. No words were needed, just the steady rhythm of our heartbeats with the soft rise and fall of a chest I'm cradled in.

All I could think about was her. And her lips. Her

lips took me to places I'd only dreamed of, but her tongue made me forget the world entirely.

The room was hushed and dim, the air warm with our shared heat and the faint scent of sweat, skin, and something sweeter. I closed my eyes, letting myself melt further into the safety of the moment, the kind that made her forget how many walls she used to have.

Jessica pressed a kiss to my hair.

Another on my shoulder.

Our fingers remained loosely entwined. I felt myself drifting, held, known, loved.

Sleep came softly, wrapped in the arms of a woman who had touched me deeper than any memory.

CHAPTER 4

I woke before the sun.

An old habit I'd never quite broken.

The room was still dark and quiet except for the soft rhythm of her breathing. Jessica lay on her side, curled toward me, hair a mess across the pillow, her arm draped over my waist like she'd always belonged there.

I feel something tender stir, something I once feared. I studied the curve of Jessica's cheek, the way her lashes rested against her skin, and thought, *How did I get so lucky?* None of the walls I've built matter here. Not anymore.

I don't move. I can't.

Not because I was trapped but because I was

afraid that if I shifted too much, the spell would break. That maybe this was the kind of happiness that only lasted until morning light reached the windows.

I stared at the ceiling. My hand rested on the bare skin of her back, and my fingers splayed gently between her shoulder blades. I could feel her heartbeat, steady and unguarded. It scared the hell out of me how easily she let me in. How badly I wanted to stay there.

I'd had other mornings after.

Mornings that felt like regret. Like silence. Like an escape plan forming under the covers.

But this… this didn't feel like that.

It felt like something I didn't know how to deserve.

Jessica stirred. Her eyes blinked open slowly, heavy with sleep, and when they met mine, she smiled without hesitation. No shame, no question. Just warmth.

"Hey," she whispered.

"Hey," I echoed, barely breathing the word.

She stretched a little, her fingers tracing slow, lazy lines over my ribs. "You always look at people like they might disappear."

"I don't mean to."

She smiled again, gentler this time. "I'm not going anywhere. Not unless you ask me to."

I didn't answer right away.

It wasn't that I didn't believe her.

It's just that I've learned how quickly things can fall apart. How even good intentions can turn into exit wounds. And here she was, tangled in my arms, and I couldn't help but wonder: *What if I mess this up? What if she sees all of me and changes her mind?*

But then she kissed the side of my neck, just once, and pulled me closer.

And suddenly, those thoughts faded.

We stayed like that for a long time. Wrapped in silence and breath, legs tangled under the quilt, the world outside still asleep.

Eventually, we dressed quietly, with soft smiles and a few stolen touches.

I laced up my boots while Jessica made two mugs of coffee. The smell of it filled the cabin, anchoring me back to something real. When she handed me mine, our fingers brushed, and she didn't let go right away.

"You still up for that hike?" she asked, eyes watching me like she was asking something deeper.

"Yeah," I said. "I think I need it."

The air outside was brisk, the sky pale with early light. Our boots crunched over frost-lined grass as we made our way toward the trailhead. She walked beside me without crowding, close enough to feel, not close enough to press.

The trail curved gently through the forest as if patience had carved it.

Pine needles softened our footsteps, thick on the ground, their scent rising in waves with every shift of the breeze, cool, sharp, and clean. The trees stretched tall above us, branches tangled like a cathedral made of wood and light. Some trunks were thick and ancient, their bark flaking and cracking, moss gathering at the base like green velvet.

Dappled sunlight filtered through the canopy, painting golden patches on the trail ahead. Birds chattered somewhere above us, warblers, maybe, and one, higher up, let out a long, rising call that echoed faintly through the trees.

Jessica walked just ahead of me, her hand occasionally brushing mine, her hair pulled into a loose braid that bounced against her back with every step. She stopped to take a picture of a patch of wild mushrooms, crouching low like a child discovering treasure.

I smiled and looked up. The leaves above rustled gently, and a whisper passed from tree to tree. Somewhere to the left, a chipmunk darted across the path and disappeared into a clump of ferns, tail flicking like a small exclamation mark.

"It smells like rain and earth and… something sweet," Jessica said, standing again.

I inhaled deeply. "Sap," I said. "That's pine pitch. The good kind. The sticky stuff that smells like cinnamon and sunlight."

She looked at me with a grin. "You say weird things like that, but somehow it always makes sense."

I shrugged. "I just listen to the forest."

A hummingbird zipped past so fast it might've been imagined, pausing for a blink on a branch before darting away.

We kept walking deeper into the woods, the world narrowing to just the crunch of gravel beneath our boots, the call-and-answer of birdsong, and the green breath of trees pressing in from all sides.

We didn't talk much at first. That kind of silence, the good kind, had grown between us like a shared language.

Halfway up the ridge, she grabbed my hand.

It isn't a question, it's a statement.

I looked over at her. She was windblown and red-cheeked and alive in a way I didn't know I'd needed to see.

"You okay?" she asked.

I stopped walking.

She turned to me, searching my face.

"I don't do this," I said softly. "I don't let people in this easily."

"I know," she said. "You didn't."

"I did with you."

Jessica didn't move. Didn't speak for a moment. Then she stepped closer and pressed her forehead to mine.

"Good," she whispered. "Because I've been falling since the first message. I didn't know how to land until now."

My chest ached in a good way.

So I kissed her.

Her lips are soft. I grab her hand, and we walk, but it feels like the ground has shifted under me.

The trees sway gently above us, chipmunks darting through the underbrush, birds calling out like the world is somehow lighter than it was ten minutes ago. But inside me? Everything feels raw. Like I've cracked open something I've spent years keeping sealed tight.

I told her. I *told her* that I don't let people in. That it's easier to stay behind the walls, to pretend I'm fine, to keep control. I've always thought that was a strength, keeping things close, never needing anyone. But when I looked at her, really looked at her... I didn't want to lie anymore.

She didn't flinch. She didn't try to fix it or change the subject. She just... listened. And something about that undid me more than any dramatic gesture ever could.

She's walking beside me now, quietly, like she knows I need the silence to breathe, but not the kind that leaves you feeling alone. The kind that says *I'm here. I'm still here.*

I don't know what comes next. I'm still scared. I'm still halfway ready to bolt at the first sign of hurt. But for the first time in a long time... I'm also curious.

What if letting someone in doesn't mean losing myself?

What if...just maybe... she's not here to break me, but to show me what it feels like to be held?

And damn it... what if I want that?

We stopped where the trees opened up just enough to let the sunlight fall across a mossy outcrop. It isn't a dramatic overlook, no sweeping valley or postcard moment, just quiet, still, and enough.

Jessica sat first, brushing a few pine needles off the rock beside her. I joined her without asking, letting my backpack slide to the ground with a soft thud. We hadn't said much for the last mile, and I didn't mind. The silence between us wasn't heavy. It felt earned.

She pulled her knees up to her chest, arms wrapped around them loosely.

"This trail reminds me of a time when I was sixteen," she said, eyes on a patch of sunlight ahead of us, "I spent a summer living with my aunt in northern Arizona. My mom had... stuff going on, and I guess I did too, but nobody knew how to talk about it."

I turned slightly toward her but didn't say anything. Just waited.

"My aunt had this hiking trail behind her house," she went on. "It wasn't long. Maybe a mile or two. But I used to walk it every morning before anyone woke up. Same path, every day, like it would eventually lead somewhere new if I just kept going long enough."

She paused and picked at a piece of bark wedged into her boot tread.

"I think that was the first time I realized I didn't want to go back. Not just to my mom's house, but... to pretend I was fine all the time. It was when my mom went off her meds again."

I didn't move. Didn't react. Just listened.

"She'd been stable and managing herself well for almost three years. I really believed it was going to stick that time. I think I wanted it more than she did."

Her voice was calm, almost clinical, but her hands were restless, fingers picking at the seam of her hiking pants.

"There was this one night," she continued, eyes fixed somewhere past the trees, "I found her on the kitchen floor. Oven still on. A cigarette was burning in the sink. I was the one who cleaned it up, turned everything off, and got her to bed. I didn't tell anyone. Just... handled it. I had to do that a lot."

I swallowed but didn't speak. My instinct was to say something soothing, but I knew better. This wasn't about comfort. This was about *truth*.

"She went to an inpatient treatment the next week," Jessica added, letting out a slow breath. "And I got shipped off to my aunt's for the summer like I was the one who'd done something wrong."

That landed. Not bitter. Just worn. Like it was a

story she'd folded and unfolded too many times to keep the edges crisp.

"That trail behind my aunt's house," she said, finally glancing at me, "it was the only place I didn't feel like a problem. Like someone's burden."

I reached out and brushed my knuckles against the back of her hand. Not demanding. Just there.

"You weren't," I said quietly. "You're not."

Her mouth curved into the kind of smile that says *thank you*, even if the words never come.

"Yeah," she said. "But it took me a long time to believe that."

She leaned her head lightly against my shoulder, and I let her stay there, the wind threading through the trees like it was letting us be.

Her voice wasn't shaking. If anything, it was calm. It was as if she'd rehearsed it, but never actually said it out loud before.

"I'm sorry," I said softly, meaning it but also knowing it wasn't enough.

She shook her head. "You don't have to be. I'm okay now. It just took a while to stop walking in circles."

I reached out just enough for my fingers to brush hers.

"You don't have to walk it alone anymore."

She looked at me then, really looked at me, and gave me a smile that didn't need translation. Quiet. Grateful. Brave.

"Good," she said. "Because I really hate getting lost."

CHAPTER 5

$\mathcal{W}$e reached the top just as the sun broke over the horizon.

The lake below glimmered like spilled gold. Pines stretched in every direction, and the sky turned that aching kind of blue you only get in the cold, sharp, endless, quiet.

Jessica stood just ahead of me, her hair caught in the wind, cheeks flushed from the climb. She turned slowly, eyes wide.

"God," she breathed. "It's like the whole world just… stopped."

I watched her instead of the view.

"I know," I murmured.

She took my hand again, then led me a few feet off the trail to a flat boulder warmed by the first light of day. We sat side by side, legs stretched out, our shoulders brushing.

"You always live like you're waiting for the ground to give out," she said softly.

I didn't answer right away. My eyes stayed on the lake, but my heart was somewhere in my throat.

"I was engaged once," I say, the words catching in my throat. "Years ago. Not many people know that. I don't like to bring it up. It's not a secret, just... a scar I keep under long sleeves."

Jessica didn't move, didn't interrupt.

"Her name was Lila. We met in grad school. She was bold, funny, and absolutely nothing like me. The kind of person who could walk into a room and rearrange the mood just by being there. She liked loud music and group brunches and always told stories with her hands. She made me feel interesting, which, at the time, felt a lot like love." I gazed down, looking at the dirt.

"She was the kind of woman who *chose* people fully and without hesitation. And for a while, she chose me. But I think I wore her down.

It didn't happen all at once. At first, she called my quiet 'mysterious' and said it was refreshing that I didn't over-share. But somewhere between months eight and fifteen, it stopped being refreshing. She started asking more questions, and I didn't know how to answer about my past, my feelings, and what I *wanted*. And the more she asked, the more I pulled back. Not to punish her. Just... out of habit.

That's the part I hate the most. I didn't push her away with some dramatic betrayal. I did it slowly. Quietly. By being too careful. By never letting her *really* see me.

And one Tuesday morning, while I was in the shower, of all things, she left. No fight. No warning. Just a handwritten note on the counter, and her key resting in the sink. Said I was too hard to reach. Too quiet. That I held her at arm's length and called it love."

Jessica looked over, and I could feel her eyes on me like sunlight.

"I don't think I ever stopped asking myself if she was right," I added. "If the way I love is just... too hard to feel."

Jessica reached over and touched my jaw, guiding my face toward hers.

"At first, I tried to be angry. I told myself she had given up. That she didn't understand me, that maybe she didn't have the patience to love someone like me. But deep down, I knew. She tried. Harder than I did. And I met her halfway for a while, but never all the way. I loved her. But I didn't know how to *show* it without feeling like I was handing her pieces of me. I hadn't even looked at myself. So I told myself I'd do better next time. If there ever was a next time."

"You don't love wrong," she said. "You love carefully. That's not the same thing."

I closed my eyes, holding still under her touch.

"I feel you," she whispered. "Every word you don't say. Every silence. I feel all of it."

When I opened my eyes, she was so close. And I was done pretending I didn't need her to see me.

So I kissed her.

Not with restraint this time. Not with hesitation.

I kissed her like she'd just unlatched something in me I didn't even know was locked.

She responded with a soft gasp, her arms moving to my neck, wrapping around me as she pulled me closer. The cold air disappeared. All I felt was her, warm, alive, anchoring me to the present like nothing ever had.

We broke the kiss only to breathe. Our foreheads rested together, breath mingling in the cold morning air.

I kiss her again, softer this time, then again, slower still, learning the shape of her mouth, the way her breath caught when my lips wandered to her jaw. Jessica's hands slid into my hair, tugging gently, pulling me back to her lips with a hunger that made my chest tighten.

My fingertips grazed the line of her ribs, hesitant at first, feeling the shiver that ran through her. She whispered my name like it was something she'd been holding back for years.

We paused, foreheads pressed together once more, both of us trembling, not from the cold but from the weight of what waited between us. Her thumb brushed over my lips, and she smiled.

And then she tugged my flannel shirt free from my jeans, fingers slipping under to touch bare skin.

My breath caught at the warmth of her hand. I kiss her again, deeper now, and she answers with a soft gasp, tugging me closer by my shirt. For a long moment, we didn't move past that, just the slow ache of mouths meeting and parting, her hands sliding up my spine beneath the fabric.

"Here?" I ask, breath catching.

She smiled, lips brushing mine. "Here. With the sky above us."

We found a soft patch of moss between the stone and the pine needles. She stretched out on my jacket, pulling me down with her, but neither of us rushed. I kiss her again and again, over her mouth, her cheek, the hollow of her throat. She sighs my name, her hands roaming my back like she was learning every line by touch. I let my lips wander down to her collarbone, tasting the salt of her skin before coming back up to find her mouth again.

There was no urgency.

Just the slow undoing of fear.

She touched me with reverence, kissed me with trust, and undressed me like I was something sacred.

I took my time with her, not rushing, not claiming, just appreciating. My hand finds the curve of her breasts, fingers spreading gently as I cup her softness. Her skin is warm beneath my touch, and I can feel her heartbeat, steady but growing faster, like her body is responding before her voice can.

I took my time, letting my fingers linger at the edge of her shirt, waiting until she lifted her arms for me to slip it free. My hands moved slowly, brushing along her arms as I eased the fabric away. She returns the gesture, sliding my flannel from my shoulders, her palms exploring me as if she'd been waiting her whole life to touch me like this.

I trail kisses across her chest, slow and unhurried, letting my lips reach her breast. I pause, breathing her in, the scent of her skin, the faint sweetness of warmth and desire. I press a kiss over her heart first, then lower, brushing my lips over her nipple tenderly, teasingly, and feel her shiver beneath me.

She sighs my name, her back arching as I take her into my mouth. I move my tongue gently, then circle it more slowly, letting her reactions guide me. My hand moves to her other breast, tracing delicate patterns with my fingers as I give each one equal devotion.

And when I enter her, she soaks my fingers with her excitement. It wasn't about heat or hunger.

It was about belonging.

There's something sacred about the moment my fingers slipped inside her, not just the physical warmth or wetness that greets you, but the way her breath catches, how her hand tightens on my arm, her body arching toward me like it's never felt more alive.

I feel everything. The way her softness draws me in, the way her body responds like it's speaking a language only the two of you understand. It's not just touch; it's listening to your skin. The tension she thrusts once, twice, over and again, the sighs, and the shivers. Her pleasure builds under my fingertips, and it fills me, too; my heartbeat syncs with hers.

Her fingers tangle in my hair, her back arches

beneath me, and I whisper her name against her neck like a promise I didn't want to break.

Her hand leaves my hair and enters me. Everything inside me quiets and ignites at once. The world narrows, and she explores me like she's memorizing a secret only I can carry.

It's overwhelming in the most beautiful ways. I instinctively part my thighs for her; my body seems designed to open for her. Each movement of her hand sends ripples through me, pleasures blooming in waves I can't control. She knows just where to press, how to curve, how to pause and build again like she's reading the tremble in my breath and responding with intention.

I cry out her name as my body trembles.

And she watches me. God, the way she watches me like she's falling in love with every sound I make, every gasp, every twitch of my hips. Her mouth finds my skin while her fingers keep coaxing me open, drawing me deeper into a space where nothing exists but her and this.

We moved together with the rhythm of wind in trees, steady, grounding, eternal.

My body starts to lose control. I hold onto her like I'm coming apart in the hands of the only person

I want to put me back together. Her tongue, oh God, her tongue, it makes my body sing.

When it's over, I rest my head on her chest, her heartbeat thudding strong beneath my ear.

"I've never felt like this," I said.

Jessica's fingers combed gently through my hair. "Me neither."

We lay there as the world kept spinning, the ridge holding us, the sun watching like it knew something we hadn't yet.

And for the first time in a long time, I didn't feel afraid.

I felt found. I found the woman whose kisses felt like a promise.

"You were the one who wanted to keep climbing," I teased, brushing my hand along her thigh.

She grinned. "Worth it."

She paused, then tilted her head toward the hallway. "You know what I could go for?"

I raised an eyebrow. "What's that?"

"A bath. A big, ridiculous bubble bath. Tell me this place has one of those clawfoot tubs in the back."

"It does."

"Her eyes widened slightly. "There's still hot water?"

"Yeah," I said. "The place runs on propane. We're lucky."

We lit the last two candles in the bathroom and filled the clawfoot tub with water warm enough to melt away the rest of the night.

I ran the water while Jessica poured the bubbles in with reckless abandon, laughing as they multiplied far beyond what was probably reasonable. When she started stripping, I had to lean on the sink to steady my heart.

She stepped in first, sighing dramatically as she sank into the foam. "Oh my god. I want to marry this tub."

I splashed her lightly, and she gasped, swatting at me through the bubbles, laughing until I caught her wrist and kissed her wet palm.

I smiled, slower, deeper. "Jealous already."

I undressed quietly, her gaze following every motion. I was still getting used to being seen. Not just touched, *seen*.

But she didn't look at me like I was a thing to take. She looked like I was something she got to keep.

I joined her slowly, sinking in behind her. She rested against me, her back against my chest, her legs tangled with mine beneath the water. For a while, I just held her, kissing the damp strands of hair at her temple, breathing her in while the storm tapped the windows like a distant heartbeat. The bubbles rose around us, soft and ridiculous and perfect.

She let out a long, contented breath. "This is heaven."

My arms slid around her waist, bubbles piling up on my arms. "You make it feel like heaven."

Her fingers intertwined with mine under the water. "You don't talk much, but when you do have something to say, I like it."

"I mean it."

She turned slightly, just enough to press a kiss to my collarbone. "I know."

The water cradled us, soft with lavender-scented bubbles that clung to our skin like silk. I press my chest to her back, tangle our legs beneath the water, and rest her head on my shoulder. The candlelight flickers, casting golden shadows over her collarbone, the steam curling around us like we're in our own world.

She caught one of my hands under the bubbles, threading her fingers with mine. Her lips brushed my knuckles, a soft kiss that made my chest tighten before I let my hand drift lower again. My hands begin innocently, gliding along her arms, up to her shoulders, then slipping beneath the surface to trace the curve of her waist, then back up to cup her breasts. Her breath catches just slightly, and I smile against her neck, pressing a slow kiss there, a promise. She tilts her head to give me more.

Her nipples harden under my touch, and I take my time, rolling them between my fingers, teasing them until her breath turns shaky. She tilts her head back against my shoulder, and a moan escapes her slightly parted lips, eyes closed like she's giving herself over completely. I kiss her neck slowly, then bite gently just below her ear.

My fingers drift lower, sliding over the softness of her belly, then between her thighs. She opens for me without a word, like her body already knows what mine is asking, and I find her warm, wet, and aching. My fingers move with purpose now, circling her clit in slow, deliberate motions. Jessica lets out a moan, low and breathless, hips rising to meet the rhythm I give her. The water laps around us, her hips shifting with each careful movement of my hand.

She reaches back blindly and finds my thigh beneath the bubbles, her hand exploring now, her touch deliberate, echoing mine, her fingers finding me just as eager. She thrusts her fingers inside me, firm and slow. I gasp softly against her skin, and she smiles. We fall into a rhythm, wet skin sliding, moans echoing off the tile, a give and take of sighs and searching fingers, pleasure rippling through the water between our bodies. Her back arches, her fingers pump inside me as mine curl inside her, and it's not just about release but about being completely open, vulnerable, and seen.

Her fingers found that spot, the one that makes me clamp down my jaw and throw my head back, and I yell out, "Yes, oh fuck, yes." She was thrusting into me so hard that I had to grip the edge of the tub, knocking the soap off the shelf and causing a loud crash.

"Shit," I whisper.

Jessica responds by speeding up the pace of her thrusting fingers; my legs shake at the building climax.

I whisper her name against her shoulder as we both come undone, breathless and trembling, the water sloshing gently around us.

We sit there for a long time, our bodies warm,

our hearts steady. Her skin against mine was soft and wet and real.

The water goes lukewarm, bubbles fading into scattered patches of foam, but neither of us has moved. We stay curled together, breathing slower now, our skin flushed and damp. Her fingers trace lazy circles on my thigh beneath the surface.

She tilts her head and looks up at me. I turn and kiss her. "Come on," I whisper. "Let me dry you off."

She hums contentedly and rises carefully from the tub. I follow, watching rivulets of water trace down her body, over her hips, her thighs. I grab the softest towel and wrap it around her shoulders, pulling her close. She leans into me, lips brushing mine, tasting like lavender and heat.

I dried her slowly, kissing droplets of water as they trailed down her skin. One at her collarbone, another at her shoulder. She laughed softly, tugging the towel from my hands and pulling me into another kiss.

In the bedroom, the sheets are cool against our still-warm skin. We fall into them together, limbs tangling easily as we've always known how to fit. We linger there, mouths brushing, trading soft kisses and whispers. Her hands moved in my hair, down my spine, each touch hesitant at first, then bolder, until I forgot the coolness of the sheets and knew only her warmth. I kiss her slowly now, unhurried, taking my time to explore her mouth, her breath, her softness beneath me. The intensity from the bath has melted into something sweeter, no less charged but quieter, more reverent.

She's curled against me now, her leg draped over mine, her cheek resting just below my collarbone. My fingers move slowly through her damp hair, and the candlelight casts a golden hush across the room. For a while, we say nothing. Just the quiet sound of our breathing. The soft comfort of skin against skin.

Then, her voice breaks the silence, quiet, a little hoarse.

"I wasn't sure I'd ever feel this again," she says. "Not just the sex, but...this. Safety. Being wanted without feeling like I have to perform or protect myself."

I swallow hard. "Yeah," I whisper, kissing the top of her head. "I know that feeling too well."

She shifts just enough to look up at me, her eyes a little glassy in the flickering light. "You didn't rush me. You didn't take. You gave, and I came to you. I don't think I knew how much I needed that."

I hold her tighter. "You never have to earn being

touched with love. You never have to apologize for wanting softness. For needing to feel seen."

Her hand brushes along my ribs, light as a breath. "I have felt touched before, but never like that."

"You are," I say firmly now. "You're *everything*. Every reaction, every breath, every sigh, I wanted all of it because it was you. Because you trusted me with it."

She lets out a shaky laugh. "You're going to make me cry."

"Then cry," I whisper. "And I'll still be right here."

And she does, just a little. Tears that aren't sad but releasing. Tears that speak of all the times she held herself alone when she needed someone's arms. I kiss them away and pull her closer until there's no space between us at all.

"I don't want to be scared anymore," she says softly.

"Then let me help you feel safe. One night at a time," I whisper back. "Starting with this one."

Her fingers comb through my hair as I press kisses to her chest, her stomach, and the inside of her thigh. She sighs my name like a prayer, and I answer it with the devotion of my tongue, my hands, and the curve of my body wrapped around hers.

We take our time, again and again, between soft

laughter and whispered confessions, the kind you can only say in the hush of candlelight, in the safety of skin on skin. And when we finally settle, her head on my chest, legs still entwined, I hold her like I never want to let her go.

Because I don't.

CHAPTER 6

The last morning started softly.

Jessica is still sleeping when I slip out of bed. She kept her arm slung across my stomach all night, and I'd spent most of the hours watching the ceiling instead of sleeping, afraid that if I let myself drift off, I'd miss the feeling of her next to me.

In the kitchen, I poured the coffee and stirred in honey, my movements too quiet in the stillness. The smell of pine crept in through the cracked window. The fire had gone low, just a soft hum of embers now.

I kept replaying that moment from earlier, the one I couldn't quite shake.

Jessica had stirred before sunrise, her voice still groggy with sleep. She'd reached for me, not just physically, but emotionally. Whispered something, half-laughed, half-serious:

"I could get used to this."

And me? I smiled. Kissed the top of her head. Said something like, "Yeah, it's been nice."

That was my first mistake.

The second was not asking her to say more, not telling her what it meant to me, too, not letting her see that my chest was burning with hope and fear in equal measure.

So now I stood alone in the quiet, holding a warm mug and the echo of her words, gentle, brave, and met with a wall.

I didn't mean to pull away. I just... did like muscle memory.

She walks into the kitchen a few minutes later, rubbing her eyes and tugging my hoodie tighter around herself. She looked so soft in the morning light, unguarded, sweet, honest, and for a second, I forgot how to breathe.

"Hey," she said quietly. "You okay?"

I nodded. "Yeah. Just... thinking."

Her gaze held mine a beat longer than usual. "About anything in particular?"

"Not really."

The answer comes too fast, too practiced.

Jessica didn't push. She just nodded and moved to the sink to wash her face. But the air shifted, barely, but I felt it like the warmth between us had taken a cautious step back.

I hated how quickly I let that happen.

We pack a small lunch and leave the cabin just before noon. The sun had come back after the storm, glinting off the lake in little flashes of silver. The trail around the water was easy, long, winding, and beautiful.

But we barely spoke.

She walked a few paces ahead at first, her hands tucked deep into the pocket of my hoodie. I caught up now and then, offered a word or two, and pointed out a bird, a trail marker, and a set of footprints in the mud.

But she didn't tease me like she usually did.

Didn't ask if I'd brought snacks.

Didn't reach for my hand.

Didn't insist on taking a silly selfie, even when the light was perfect.

And me? I stayed quiet. I told myself I was giving her space. But maybe I was just waiting for her to make it easy again.

That was my third mistake.

Because I'd already made it more complicated

than it had to be.

She'd offered me something real this morning, something small but vulnerable, and I'd deflected it like I always do. It wasn't cold or cruel, but the distance was still enough to be felt.

Not because I didn't care.

Because I cared too much.

The silence between us was thick with everything I hadn't said. Everything she hadn't asked twice.

Near the far curve of the lake, she stopped and stared out over the water, arms crossed loosely in front of her. I slowed beside her, unsure whether I should speak.

Her voice broke through first, soft. "You seemed... somewhere else this morning."

I looked out at the lake with her. "I wasn't."

"You weren't here, either."

That one landed. Not sharp, but heavy.

I turned toward her and tried to explain. "I didn't mean to be distant."

She nodded, jaw tensing slightly. "I know. It just... felt like maybe I made it too real."

Her honesty made my chest ache. "No," I said quickly. "That's not it."

Jessica glanced at me, eyes searching. "Then what is it?"

I hesitated. The truth felt too big to say and too important not to. "I'm still figuring out how to do this. Let someone in. Let *you* in. I want to, but sometimes it feels like I don't know how."

She nodded slowly, the tiniest breath of relief passing through her lips, but not enough to undo the ache between us.

"I just don't want to feel like a vacation," she said quietly. "Something soft and fleeting. Here today, forgotten next week."

I stepped closer, heart in my throat. "You're not."

She looked up at me then, her eyes wide and open, terrified and brave all at once. I could see her hope hiding behind the fear, begging to be chosen. "Then act like it."

She turned and walked ahead again, this time at a slower pace. Leaving space but not walking away completely.

I let her.

It wasn't because I didn't want to chase her, but because I needed to figure out how.

We stop at a sun-dappled clearing just off the trail, where the trees opened wide enough to let in warm shafts of light. A fallen log served as our bench, and a flat rock worked well enough as a table. Birds chirped overhead, and a chipmunk darted past, unbothered by the tension thickening between us.

Jessica unwrapped the sandwiches in silence, handing one to me without looking.

I muttered a soft "Thanks," our fingers brushing briefly. She pulled hers back a second too soon.

We ate slowly. The crunch of lettuce. The rustle of paper. The sound of birds and wind, and space too full of things unsaid.

I wanted to say something, anything, but everything in my head sounded either too small or too late.

Jessica took a bite, chewed carefully, then said, "The trail's not as steep as I thought it'd be."

"Yeah." I nodded. "It's... nice. Quiet."

She looked up at the trees. "Peaceful, I guess."

"Mhm."

Another pause. Another bite. Another silence that was heavy enough to bend the branches around us.

Then she said, almost too softly, "You're quiet today."

I swallowed. "So are you."

Jessica gave a tiny shrug, her gaze still down. "I just don't want to say the wrong thing."

"That makes two of us."

She smiled, faint and sad. "I hate when it's like this."

"Me too," I said. "But I don't want to fight."

"I don't either," she whispered, her hands tightening around the sandwich. "I just... sometimes I feel like I'm the only one reaching."

The words settled into the clearing like truth, plain and solid.

I looked at her, wanting to say that she wasn't. That I was reaching too. Just differently. Quietly. Terrified. But all I said was, "I know."

Jessica stood slowly, brushing crumbs from her lap.

We walked again for a while. Not far. Not close.

Near a bend in the trail where the trees parted and let the sun spill down like a golden invitation, she stopped and turned toward me.

"I think I'm going to keep walking for a bit," she said softly. "Alone."

I froze, unsure how to read her face. She wasn't angry. Just tired. Distant. Like she'd taken a small step back inside herself and didn't know how to come out again.

"I just need a little space to think," she added gently. "I'll meet you back at the cabin later, okay?"

I wanted to ask why. Suppose I'd said something wrong. To wonder if this was the part where every-thing started to unravel.

But something in her voice told me this wasn't about me, at least not entirely. This was about how we both kept brushing against something real and stepping back before it hurt.

So I nodded. Even though it felt like the trail suddenly forked in two.

"Okay," I said. "I'll put on some tea when I get back."

She gives me a faint smile, grateful, maybe a little sad, then leans in and presses a quick kiss to my cheek.

And then she turned, her boots crunching down the path, fading into sunlight and birdsong and the space I hadn't meant to put between us.

I stand there for a while after she disappears, surrounded by wind and pine and the quiet ache of letting someone walk away without chasing after them.

Then I started back toward the cabin, already feeling the words I hadn't said lining up in my chest, asking to be let out before it was too late.

At the small kitchen table, I cracked the window just enough to let in the smell of wood smoke and damp earth. The fire had burned low, now reduced to just glowing embers.

Jessica wasn't back yet.

I told myself I wasn't watching the clock. But I knew. I felt every minute like a weight pressing down on my ribs.

My journal lay open in front of me. I'd written half a sentence fifteen minutes ago and couldn't bring myself to finish it.

I don't know how to be close without feeling like I might break.

I stared at the ink, fingers resting on the pen. I didn't know if I was talking about myself or the people I kept trying not to lose.

I'd told Jessica I was bad at this: relationships, vulnerability, and being known.

She hadn't argued, which was almost worse than if she had.

Because she wasn't wrong to need more. To ask for more.

And today, I'd felt her retreat.

"It wasn't anger or even disappointment, just quiet."

As if she were testing to see if I'd notice. Whether I'd follow.

And I had.

God, I had.

I pressed the pen to the page again.

> *I think I've spent so long guarding the softest parts of myself that I forgot how to offer them to anyone else. I've called it strength. Independence. But the truth is, I've just been afraid.*
>
> *Afraid that if someone really saw all of me, they'd leave.*
>
> *But Jessica saw the cracks. And she stayed. And I gave her silence in return.*

I stopped writing. Shut the journal, as if I could trap the truth inside it before it got too loud.

But it was already loud.

I was going to tell her everything.

Not just *I'm sorry.*

But *why* did I make it so hard for her to stay close? Why was I pretending that distance was the same as safety?

Maybe it would come out awkward. Maybe I'd cry. Maybe I'd stumble.

But this time, I wasn't going to let the silence speak for me.

CHAPTER 7

I heard the crunch of her boots before I saw her.

She walked up the steps slower than usual, like she hadn't quite decided how the rest of the evening would go. I stayed near the stove. Journal closed, fingers curled around a lukewarm mug I'd forgotten to drink.

The door creaked open.

Jessica steps inside, cheeks flushed from the cold, eyes cautious but not closed.

"Hey," she said softly, brushing snow from her sleeves.

"Hey," I echoed, my voice coming out smaller than I intended. I set the mug down and took a breath. "Can I say something before you sit down? Before it gets too easy not to?"

She nodded, one hand still holding the edge of the door like she wasn't sure if she was staying or just pausing.

"I'm sorry," I said, voice low. "For earlier. For all of it."

Her brow knitted gently. She didn't interrupt, didn't move.

I pressed forward, the words fragile but finally free.

"I've spent a long time convincing myself that keeping people at arm's length was... smart. Safe. And most days, I actually believed it. That if I didn't ask for too much or show too much, I couldn't lose anything."

I let out a breath. It shook.

"But then you showed up, really showed up, and I did the thing I always do. I pulled back just enough to pretend I wasn't afraid."

She stepped farther inside, closing the door behind her with a quiet click.

"I *am* afraid, Jess," I said, locking eyes with her. "Not of you. Of what it means to let someone in and not have an exit strategy. Of what happens if you see all the ways I'm still figuring this out and decide it's too much."

Jessica drops her bag on the bench and walks toward me slowly as if the space between us had already forgiven me.

"I'm not asking you to be perfect," she said, her voice gentler than I deserved. "I just need you to show up. Not halfway. Not behind walls. Just... here."

"I want to," I said. "I'm trying. Even if it's clumsy and awkward, and I don't always get it right, I want to be here. With you."

That was it—no grand gesture, no sweeping music. Just the two of us standing in the warmth of this cabin with miles of quiet honesty stretched between us.

She stepped close and wrapped her arms around me, head tucked against my shoulder.

"I wasn't going to walk away," she whispered. "I just needed to know you wouldn't let me disappear."

I held her tighter, my chest loosening for the first time all day.

"I won't," I said. "Not anymore."

"Now, can I ask you something?" she said finally.

I looked up. "Yeah."

Her eyes looked into mine, sharp but not angry. Just... aching.

"If this is just a mountain thing," she said, "tell me now."

My stomach dropped.

Her voice didn't waver, but I could still hear it. That quiver underneath, trying not to show how much the question cost her.

"It's not," I said.

Her eyes searched mine.

"This is more than that," I added, quieter now. "I just... don't always know how to say it."

She held still, shoulders tight. "Try."

So I did.

"I don't let people in," I said, voice lower than I meant. "I never have. I keep things tight and controlled. I let them think they know me without really letting them *see* me."

Her lips parted, but she didn't interrupt.

"But you," I breathed. "You're already inside. And that scares the hell out of me."

I took a step closer. "Because when something's real, it has the power to wreck you."

Her eyes shimmer, not with tears, not quite, but with something more dangerous: relief.

"Siobhan," she whispered, as if my name meant something.

I reached for her hand, and she let me take it.

"I didn't say the right thing this morning," I said. "I didn't say anything at all. But you need to know, there is no one else in my life who makes me want to stay."

Jessica's fingers gripped mine like they needed to anchor both of us.

"I didn't want a fling," she said. "I came here hoping it could be more. Hoping you could be more."

I nodded slowly. "I want more."

She stepped forward into my chest, resting her forehead against me. My arms slid around her waist, and for the first time that day, I exhaled fully.

"I don't need perfect words," she whispered. "I just need the truth."

"Then here it is," I said, my voice rough with honesty. "I'm in this. Whatever it looks like when we go home. I'm not letting this end here."

Jessica leaned back just enough to look up at me. "Good. Because I was already planning the next trip."

I felt myself start to smile a little. "You don't like to waste time, do you?"

"Not when it matters."

We sit on the couch, just quiet. Jessica had her legs draped over mine, a blanket pulled across both our laps. The fire was low, almost gone, but its warmth still clung to the room.

The silence was comfortable. And I thought maybe the night would end just like that—us, in this small stillness that felt like more than enough.

But then she looked up at me, her voice barely above a whisper.

"Can I ask you something a little heavy?"

I nodded, brushing my thumb along her shin. "You can ask me anything."

She hesitated. Then, carefully: "Do you ever think about our future? Like… what could this become?"

The air doesn't shift.

I do.

She wasn't asking for a ring or a timeline. I knew that. But my chest tightened all the same because that question meant she was already thinking about it. And I'd spent so long being afraid to.

I didn't answer right away. I looked at our hands, hers resting in mine, soft and certain. And I thought of all the quiet ways she'd already become part of my life. Not with noise. But with presence.

So I told her the truth.

"Yeah," I said. "I think about it more than I know how to admit."

Her eyes met mine, open, hopeful, but holding back just a little, like she didn't want to push.

I kept going. Slow. Honest.

"I think about waking up with you beside me, not just here, but at home too. I think about mornings when we fight over the last piece of toast and laugh about it five minutes later. I think about having to stop by the store on the way home and texting you if we need milk."

Jessica blinked, her lips curling into the start of a smile. "So… toast and milk?"

I grinned. "And you're humming in the kitchen while you burn something you swore you couldn't mess up."

She laughed then, full and warm, leaning her head against my shoulder. "I love that that's what you see."

"I see a life," I said. "Not just a weekend. Not just this cabin. You. In my world. In the quiet parts. The ordinary."

Jessica was quiet for a moment, her fingers moving slowly across my wrist.

"I don't need a promise," she said. "I just needed to know you think about it too."

I kissed the top of her head. "I do. More than I should. Less than you deserve."

Her hand found mine under the blanket again, and she squeezed it.

And there, on that couch, with the fire almost out and the world too far away to matter, I finally let myself believe in a future I used to think was meant for other people.

Now I knew better.

It was meant for us.

And somehow, just like that, the room felt warm again.

Not because of the fire, but because we'd finally stopped holding back.

CHAPTER 8

*T*he morning after everything cleared between us, we packed light and set out early.

Jessica's fingers brushed mine as we walked the trail, no hesitation this time, no stolen glances to check the distance. Just her, beside me, steady as breath.

We hiked in easy silence, not because there was nothing to say but because we finally didn't need to fill the space.

The air was damp, with the remnants of the storm still present. Ferns hung heavy on the edges of the path, the scent of wet pine thick in the air. Jessica's laughter drifted through the trees now and then, especially when I slipped on a patch of mud and tried to play it off like nothing happened.

But it wasn't until we reached the waterfall that time seemed to pause.

It was taller than I expected. It's not huge, nothing dramatic, but beautiful. A silver stream poured over dark stone, crashing into a shallow pool surrounded by moss and sun-speckled rock. Mist hung in the air like a veil.

Jessica walked to the edge and stood there, hands on her hips, eyes wide with awe. Her hair whipped around in the wind. My hoodie still swallowed her frame, and I couldn't stop staring at her.

She turned, her gaze locking with mine.

"You're staring again," she said, smiling.

"I can't help it."

Her smile softened, and she crossed back to me.

This time, when I kissed her, it wasn't tentative. It wasn't questioning.

It was full.

Intentional.

She responded with a quiet sound that pierced me straight through. Her hands tangled in the collar of my flannel, pulling me closer. The world blurred around us, water crashing behind, birds singing overhead, everything else falling away.

We broke the kiss only to breathe.

I pressed my forehead to hers. "Stay close," I whispered.

She nodded, her hands sliding down my chest, warm and steady. "Always."

The cold air nips at our skin, but we don't feel it, not with how her lips crash into mine beneath the pine trees, mouths parting, breaths stolen. Her arms wrap around me tightly, her hands tangling in my hair, mine gripping her hips. The forest is quiet, but we aren't; we are gasping, kissing like we've been waiting all day to break open.

I let go of her hand and caught her by the hips.

She blinked in surprise, her smile faltering for a heartbeat. "Siobhan?"

I didn't answer. I just backed her up slowly, step by step, until her back met the broad trunk of a pine tree. Moss cushioned one side, bark rough against her shoulder blades. Her breath caught in her throat.

"What are you..."

I pressed in, one hand cradling her jaw, the other at her waist.

Her sentence melted into a gasp when I kissed her.

Not soft. Not hesitant.

Hungry.

My body covered hers, not to overpower, but to *anchor*. To ensure she felt everything, I was finally willing to give.

Her fingers dug into my back, pulling me closer. Her mouth opened to mine, and we kissed like we were chasing something we'd been afraid to name.

I pulled back just enough to speak, my forehead resting against hers, breath ragged.

"I can't keep pretending I don't want you this much."

Jessica looked up at me, eyes wide, lips kiss-bruised. "Then don't."

My hand slid under her hoodie, fingers brushing her bare skin, the heat of her making my head spin.

"Tell me to stop," I whispered.

She shook her head. "I want this. I want *you*."

I kissed her again, harder this time, one thigh pressing between hers, our bodies aligned, breath synced and building. Her hands threaded into my hair, pulling me deeper, closer *home*.

She moans against my mouth, her teeth grazing my lower lip, and that's it, we need to move. Now.

"Back to the cabin," she breathes against my neck.

"Run," I whisper.

We stumble over roots and patches of snow, laughter tangled with lust as we race down the hill, hands brushing, then gripping tight. She throws open the door first, and I follow. The cabin is cool and dim, the fireplace dark.

I drop to my knees, striking a match with shaking fingers. As flames begin to catch, she comes up behind me, pulling me into her, kissing the back of my neck, and tugging off her jacket and shirt. The heat from the fire meets the heat already rising between us.

She turns and pulls me down to the floor with her mouth crashing again. Clothes are peeled off in clumsy, desperate movements, sweaters, jeans, and underwear until skin meets skin, bare and burning.

For a moment, we just stare, skin bared in firelight, taking each other in. I let my palms roam over the curve of her shoulders, the line of her waist, memorizing every inch before I bent to kiss her collarbone, her stomach, her hipbone, each kiss a slow claim.

"I want you," she breathes.

I roll her onto her back on the thick rug, the firelight dancing across her chest. She opens for me without a word, her thighs parting, hands pulling me down. I run my bare hands over her warm skin, and her nipples hardened under my touch; I cupped her breast, gently squeezing.

My hand drifted lower, but not all at once. I traced lazy circles along her hip, the inside of her thigh, watching the way her body responded before I finally slid my fingers between her legs.

My hand lingers over the curves of her body, slipping below her waist. I close my eyes and press my head into her shoulder. *My God, this woman drives me insane! I want to feel every inch of her and taste her.*

"Siobhan, please," she whispers.

My fingers find her first, soaked, ready, and she cries out into my mouth as I kiss her deeply, thrusting into her with aching need. She grabs my hand and pulls me out, drawing my hand up her body and putting my fingers in her mouth, sucking them. She moans softly, "Mmm." I pulled my hand away and found her again, slowly thrusting my fingers inside her. She grabbed my arm, her hips bucking to meet me, another hand clutching my back, nails dragging along my skin as I built a rhythm. My arm will bear the marks tomorrow. She's gasping now, louder, her head reclined and her legs wrapped tight around me.

We kissed until our lips ached, both of us gasping, our chests slick with sweat. She pulls back just enough to look at me, her eyes burning, and only then does she push me gently onto my back and climb over me, claiming her turn.

Jessica, taking control, slides a hand between my legs. I rock my hips as I lock eyes with her. The world around me disappears. She holds my gaze. At this moment, my body relaxes into her. She pumps her fingers into me. I can feel my wetness trailing down my skin. My pussy is throbbing, pulsating waves of pleasure. I glance at her lips. I want her between my legs now. My hand grabs her head and pushes it down. Her mouth trailed lower, kissing over my ribs, my stomach, then pausing at the edge of my thigh. She stayed there a moment, breathing me in, letting me squirm before she finally pressed her lips where I needed her most.

Her lips trail down my body, tongue circling my nipple before her mouth moves lower. I groan, clutching her hair, my back arching as her tongue finds me, licks me open, and draws me higher and higher. It's messy, raw, honest, the kind of pleasure that makes your chest tighten and your eyes burn.

I reach for her, pulling her up to kiss me again, tasting myself on her lips as she sinks onto me, guiding me back inside her with one slow, perfect thrust of my fingers.

We rock together, flames flickering, bodies slick

and shaking. Her orgasm comes with a cry, raw and beautiful, and it triggers mine like a fuse, both of us trembling in each other's arms, hips still moving, kissing through it like we never want to stop.

Afterward, we collapse on the rug, tangled in blankets, legs intertwined as the fire crackles beside us. She brushes a strand of hair from my face and whispers, "That felt like something more."

I smile, still breathless. "That *was* something more."

And we lie there, warm, glowing in the firelight, and stare at each other.

We didn't rush. But it wasn't gentle, either.

It was *honest*.

She stretches beside me, still glowing in the firelight, then leans over and kisses my shoulder. "If we don't get up soon, I'm going to end up having you for dinner."

I laugh, rolling onto my side to face her. "Tempting, but I think we promised ourselves actual food."

She smirks and rises slowly, completely unashamed, slipping on my flannel shirt and nothing else. "Then come on, beautiful. Let's make something... before I decide dessert should come first."

I follow her, grinning, watching the sway of her

hips as she walks toward the kitchen. "You're lucky I like to cook hungry."

She throws a wink over her shoulder. "Oh, I plan to work up your appetite again later."

"I vote you chop vegetables," she said. "I don't trust you near a stove."

I raised a brow. "That's slander."

"You boiled pasta with the burner off yesterday."

"I was distracted."

She smirked. "By my charm?"

"By how beautiful you are."

She laughed and tossed me a cutting board. "Chop, mountain woman. Make yourself useful."

I washed the carrots, grabbed a knife, and leaned into the rhythm, watching her move around the tiny kitchen with a confidence that was entirely hers. Every once in a while, she'd glance back and shoot me a look over her shoulder. Playful. Bold.

She was messing with the sauce when I danced up behind her and wrapped my arms around her waist.

She startled slightly, then leaned back into me. "Trying to steal a taste?"

"Trying to decide if you're sweeter than the tomatoes."

She snorted. "That was awful. Try again."

I kissed the spot just beneath her ear. "You make it hard to think straight."

She froze for half a beat. Then turned in my arms and kissed me, soft, quick, tasting like garlic and wine.

"That one was better," she whispered against my mouth.

We finish the meal together, her dancing between burners and me pretending not to steal grated cheese when she wasn't looking. We set the table lazily, placing candles in chipped glass jars and using mismatched plates as if it were our fifth anniversary instead of our final night.

The food was simple. Roasted veggies, pan-seared chicken, buttery rice. Nothing fancy. But it tasted like comfort. Like home.

We sat across from each other, knees brushing under the table, wine glasses half full, the light low and golden.

Jessica chewed a bite of carrot and made a thoughtful face. "Okay, you're officially hired as my kitchen assistant."

I grinned. "'Assistant?' I echo, raising a brow.

"Maybe co-chef. But only if you keep wearing that flannel."

I leaned back on my chair, "That's what does it for you?"

She nodded, completely serious. "It's giving wilderness wife. Ten out of ten."

I laughed hard. The sound surprised me. It had been a long time since someone pulled that out of me without trying.

She watched me, eyes warm. "I love it when you laugh."

I swallowed, my heart suddenly louder than the silence around us.

"Me too," I said softly. "Especially when it's with you."

We spent the rest of dinner trading glances and small touches, brushing fingers as we cleared plates and sharing quiet smiles over candlelight. And when we finished, we didn't rush to move.

We just sat there, side by side now, sipping wine, leaning into the quiet the way you do when you know time is running out but you're not ready to let go.

Not yet.

That night, we climbed into bed together with no fanfare and no games. Her head on my chest, my fingers tracing patterns over her spine. We didn't need to speak.

We were finally aligned: body, heart, breath.

As she drifted off, her hand found mine under the blanket. She whispered something, half-sleep, half-smile.

"I don't want to go home."

I kissed the top of her head and held her tighter.

"You already are," I said.

And for once, I didn't question if I meant it.

CHAPTER 9

The last morning came too quietly.

No alarm. No urgency. Just soft light filtering through the curtains and the low creak of the cabin settling in on itself.

Jessica was already up when I rolled out of bed. She's folding blankets in the living room, her hair tied up, sleeves rolled, eyes focused like the corners of the quilt might tell her something she didn't already know.

I watched her for a moment from the hallway, one hand braced on the doorframe. She looked so at home, it hurt a little.

The last morning came too quietly.

No alarm. No urgency. Just soft light filtering

through the curtains and the low creak of the cabin settling in on itself.

I watched her for a moment from the hallway, one hand braced on the doorframe. She looked so at home, it hurt a little.

I turned and headed into the kitchen. The coffee pot groans to life, its familiar sputter filling the space as I move on autopilot—grinding beans, measuring water, pouring slowly.

Behind me, I heard her footsteps, light against the wooden floor. She paused in the doorway, taking in the room with a quiet satisfaction.

"Blankets folded. Firewood stacked. Dishes drying," she said softly. "Think we did alright."

I looked over my shoulder. She was standing still, arms crossed, watching me.

"You make a good mountain wife," I said.

She smirked. "You say that like you're surprised."

"I'm not." I turned and placed a mug on the counter in front of her. "What are you doing next weekend?"

She blinked, then smiled slowly. "Are you asking me to bring my blanket-folding skills on the road?"

"I'm asking if I can see you again."

She stepped forward, wrapping her hands around the warm mug. "You better."

We packed the car in slow motion. Neither of us said it out loud, but it was there in everything we did, in the way she placed her bag gently in the trunk, in the way I lingered by the porch steps, staring out at the lake like it might give me a reason to stay longer.

She was standing by the driver's side door, the morning light catching the edges of her hair and turning it gold where it should've been dark. She doesn't know it, but her braid is slipping loose. A few strands curl around her cheek, soft and stubborn. Like her.

She was smiling, but it was the kind of smile you give someone when you're already missing them.

And God, she was beautiful. Not in a loud way, not in a way that tried, just in a way that simply was. The kind of beauty that settles into your bones slowly until you can't remember what it felt like to be in a world where she didn't exist.

She hugged the shirt she'd slept in to her chest like she might forget it if she put it down. I wanted to tell her she could have it, that she could take any*thing she wanted.*

But I didn't.

Because the lump in my throat was too thick, and the ache in my chest had too much to say already.

I just looked at her and thought, *How did I get this lucky?*

How did someone like me, someone who takes their time and keeps their heart behind lock and key, end up with her looking at me like *this*? With her hands warm and steady on mine? With her laugh still echoing through the cabin, already a memory?

I didn't find her.

She found me.

And now I had to let her go, just for now, but everything in me screamed not to.

Not because I'm afraid she won't come back, but because I've never wanted someone to come back so much.

She reached for the car door, and I found my voice just in time.

"I want this," I said. "Not just the mountain. You."

And the way she smiled at me then, soft, certain, eyes shining like she already knew,

It wrecked me in the best way.

Jessica looked up at me. "This was supposed to be just a test run, you know. One long weekend to see if we could stand each other."

I nodded. "And now?"

She shrugged, eyes shining. "Now I don't really want to go."

I took a breath.

Jessica's mouth parted slightly like I'd caught her off guard. Then she stepped closer, slid her arms around my waist, and pressed her forehead to mine.

"Good," she whispered. "Because I've been yours since you handed me your jacket in the rain."

I kissed her once, slow, certain.

She climbs into the car. I stand by the window while she rolls it down.

"Text me when you get home," I say.

She smiles. "Try not to get that hoodie too muddy without me."

"I'll try not to."

Her car turns down the narrow dirt road, tires crunching slowly over gravel, brake lights blinking once before she disappears between the trees.

I stood there a little longer than I meant to. The wind had picked up, cold enough to bite, but I didn't move. I just listened to the sudden quiet.

No more footsteps. No more shared coffee spoons or books half-finished on the couch. Just me. And the way the air felt different now that she'd been here.

Eventually, I went inside.

The cabin already felt too still. I almost reached for her mug on the counter before remembering she'd rinsed it and set it upside down like it was a habit now.

I sat at the desk. Opened my journal one last time. No warm-up scribble. No avoidance.

Just truth.

She left this morning. Not in the way others have. Not in silence. Not in retreat. She left, knowing I wanted her to come back. And I think she will.

This weekend was something I didn't expect to be ready for. But somehow, I was. Not perfect. Not polished. But ready enough.

She doesn't just fit into my life. She makes me want to create something new, a space big enough for both of us. One that doesn't rely on distance to feel safe.

I didn't know the beginning of love could feel like this, quiet and steady. Like softness, not sacrifice. Like choosing, not chasing.

This weekend wasn't perfect. I messed up. I panicked. But I also stayed. I opened the door and let her see the parts I'd spent years guarding. And she didn't walk away.

She leaned in.

I paused, the weight of it settling into my chest, not heavy. Just real.

I've spent years pretending I didn't need what I actually ached for. But now I know: being known is scary. But being loved for all the things I never thought someone would stay for...

That's worth it.

I closed the journal slowly and let my hand rest on the cover for a moment.

And for the first time in a long, long while, I wasn't writing to make sense of loneliness.

I was writing to remember love when it shows up softly and waits for you to meet it.

Outside, the wind moved through the trees like it had somewhere to be. But I didn't.

For once, I didn't feel like I had to run.

This wasn't the end.

It was the beginning.

EPILOGUE

*I*t's been a month.

Thirty quiet mornings. A hundred text messages that always come right when I need them. Two visits, one hers, one mine, and a phone call every night that starts with "Hey" and ends with "Be safe, I miss you."

And still... I catch myself watching the door sometimes, like she might walk in, even when I know she's hours away.

I never used to do that.

I used to guard myself as if it were a matter of survival. I wore distance like armor. I kept people at a safe distance, just long enough to feel something without ever letting it matter too much.

But Jessica?

She mattered from the start.

I fought that. God, I did. I stayed quiet when I should've spoken. I pulled back when I should've leaned in. I watched her for days before I dared to really *see* her, and even longer before I let her *see* me.

But she waited. Not passively, *patiently.* With this kind of grace, I didn't know I needed until I was standing in it.

And now, a month later, I lie in bed thinking of her smile, my chest full in a way that doesn't feel dangerous anymore.

It feels *earned.*

I think about how she laughs with her whole body, how she says my name like a gift, how she still tucks one of my poems into her coat pocket and sends me pictures of it next to her coffee mug like it's something sacred.

And I'm just grateful.

Grateful, I let my guard down.

Grateful I didn't let fear choose for me.

Grateful that someone like her exists in the same world as someone like me, and somehow, she didn't just reach for me.

She stayed.

And she's still staying.

And for the first time in a long time, *so am I.*

JUST HER STORIES PUBLISHING

We hope you enjoyed the Story!

Reviews are truly gold for authors. They help new readers discover our work and keep indie stories alive. If you have a moment, I'd be so grateful if you left a quick review on Amazon or Goodreads. Even a single sentence makes a big difference. Thank you so much for your support!

Want more sapphic stories? Follow **Just Her Stories** on Facebook or visit our website for bonus chapters, sneak peeks, and extra content. www.justherstories.com

Coming Soon

Sapphic Snacks by Monet Poussay

Bite-sized, spicy romances made to savor in one

sitting. Each story takes about twenty minutes—just enough to heat up your night before bed. Whether you crave sweet flirtation, sizzling passion, or bold adventures in love, these quick reads deliver a full serving of sapphic spice on every page.

Available individually or as a series collection—indulge yourself, you deserve a midnight treat.

Beneath the Surface by Monet Poussay

A Sapphic Spicy Romance Level 4/5

Sloan Locke is part of Locke Tactical, her family's shadow business that takes on the government contracts no one else will touch. To the outside world, they're just real estate investors. In truth, their empire is built on secrets and danger.

After her twin sister is killed on their last job, Sloan retreats with her family to Colorado, desperate for a fresh start. But finding a dead man in an RV on her family's land shatters that fragile peace and raises even more questions when Rowan Thorn, a new ranch hand, seems to know things no ordinary hire should.

Rowan is unsettling, capable, and impossible to ignore. The more Sloan watches her, the deeper her suspicion grows... along with an attraction she can't fight. Desire simmers between them, slow and dangerous, pulling Sloan into a web of mistrust, grief, and heat she swore she didn't need.

As violence draws closer and secrets unravel, Sloan must decide if trusting Rowan is worth the risk, because the truth could cost her family everything. And resisting Rowan might cost her heart.

A spicy lesbian romantic thriller full of slow-burn tension, voyeuristic heat, and razor-edged suspense, perfect for readers who crave danger with their desire.

Forgotten By N.M. McCormick

A Sapphic Dystopian Fantasy - Book 1 of 3 *Under Her Land* Series

Once, Saoirse loved the Regent. Once, she was erased for it.

In UnderHerLand, *where memory is currency and obedience is survival, Saoirse's forgotten past begins to resurface. As the Sovereign's propaganda tightens its grip and The Magnus rises unchecked, rebellion stirs in the shadows.*

Saoirse should have been forgotten too—but fragments of her identity return, pulling her into a fight where loyalty is fragile and desire cuts deep. And when memory itself becomes the deadliest weapon, Saoirse must decide: will she fight for freedom, or be consumed by what she remembers?

A sapphic dystopian fantasy of love, betrayal, and rebellion—where memory is the most dangerous power of all.

The Last Sabre By N.M. McCormick

A Sapphic Urban Fantasy

In a world where evil wears human faces and blood-lines are the only shield, one woman and her venomous dragon stand between humanity and a rising darkness.

Born from a legacy of fierce female warriors known as Sabres, she was created to hunt the monsters the world refuses to see: shapeshifters, corrupted soldiers called Shades, and creatures born from the Rift itself. The Makers know her name, and they fear what sleeps in her soul.

With her dragon curled in her backpack, buried memories clawing at her mind, and a girlfriend whose supernatural gift could unravel them both, she must fight to protect the people she loves, while keeping a secret that could destroy everything.

But when an ancient darkness turns its gaze on her, the hunt becomes personal. And this time, even legacy might not be enough.

For fans of character-driven fantasy with bite, mystery, sapphic love, and dragons that don't play by the rules.

This isn't your average dragon tale; this is legacy, venom, and fire.

ABOUT THE AUTHOR

Monet Poussay is an emerging author of sapphic romance. She writes stories hat feel like whispered secrets, tender, aching, and just a little wild. Her characters find love in unlikely places and healing in unexpected ways.

When she's not writing, Monet can be found wandering through old bookstores, hiking in the mountains, or dreaming up new stories.

She lives in a quiet corner of the South and believes that some of the most powerful truths are the ones left unwritten.

Her wife, DaNeal Eberly, is the cover artist for this book—a collaboration that brings their creative visions together on the page. You can see more of her artwork on Instagram @ArtbyDaNeal

To learn more about Monet's upcoming books and other Sapphic authors, visit:

www.justherstories.com